To a little dog named Bo, who taught
us so much about the beauty of love

SIMON & SCHUSTER BOOKS FOR YOUNG READERS
An imprint of Simon & Schuster Children's Publishing Division
1230 Avenue of the Americas, New York, New York 10020
Text copyright © 2003 by Jeanne Modesitt
Illustrations copyright © 2003 by Robin Spowart
Book design by Robin Spowart and Greg Stadnyk
The text for this book is set in 15-point Dutch 809.
The illustrations are rendered in colored pencil on illustration board.
Manufactured in China
2 4 6 8 10 9 7 5 3 1
Library of Congress Cataloging-in-Publication Data
Modesitt, Jeanne.
Little Bunny's Christmas tree / [written by] Jeanne Modesitt ; [illustrated by] Robin Spowart.—1st ed.
p. cm.
Summary: Little Bunny and her family pick out the perfect Christmas tree and then decorate it together.
ISBN 0-689-84342-9
[1. Christmas trees—Fiction. 2. Christmas—Fiction. 3. Rabbits—Fiction. 4. Animals—Infancy—Fiction.] I. Spowart,
Robin, ill. II. Title.
PZ.M715 Lg 2002
[E]—dc21   2001020780

Little Bunny's Christmas Tree

by Jeanne Modesitt

illustrated by Robin Spowart

Simon & Schuster Books for Young Readers

New York London Toronto Sydney Singapore

It was the morning of Christmas Eve.
Little Bunny woke up, feeling especially happy.
This morning, she and her family were going to
pick out their Christmas tree! Little Bunny
hopped out of bed and woke up Baby Brother.

"Wake up, Baby Brother," she said. "It's time to get our Christmas tree."

Baby Brother rubbed his eyes and smiled. He crawled out of bed and put his hand into Little Bunny's. Together they went into Mama and Papa's room.

"Wake up!" said Little Bunny, giggling as she jumped on her parents' bed. "It's time to pick out our Christmas tree."

Mama and Papa opened their eyes to a smiling, eager Little Bunny before them. Mama winked and ruffled Little Bunny's ears. "Mind if we eat some breakfast first?" she asked.

"Okay," said Little Bunny. "Breakfast first, but then . . . our tree!"

Soon, Mama, Papa, Baby Brother, and Little Bunny, their tummies full of breakfast muffins, arrived at Mr. Samson's Christmas tree lot.

Papa pointed to a tall tree. "How about this one?" he asked.

Mama nodded. "It looks fine to me."

"Little Bunny? Baby Brother?" asked Papa. "What do you think?"

Little Bunny paused. "It's very nice, Papa, but I think it's too . . ."

"Big!" blurted out Baby Brother.

Little Bunny nodded. "Too big," she agreed.

"Okay," said Papa. "Let's look around some more." And the family moved on.

Moments later, Mama pointed to a tree. "I like this one," she said. "How does everyone else feel?"

Papa nodded. "I like it too," he said.

"Little Bunny? Baby Brother?" asked Mama.

Little Bunny looked up at Mama. "It's very nice, Mama, but I don't think there are enough . . ."

"Branches!" blurted out Baby Brother.

Little Bunny nodded. "Not enough branches," she agreed.

Mama smiled. "Well then, let's look some more," she said. And the family moved on.

All of a sudden, Little Bunny pointed and said, "Look!"

There in the corner of the lot, in a small pot full of dirt, stood a little, live Christmas tree.

Mr. Samson came up from behind. "Well, my goodness," he said. "You're the first one to even notice that tree. Everyone else walks right past it, like it isn't even there. Too small, I guess."

Little Bunny went up to the tree. "Look," she said, turning back to her family, her eyes shining. "It's as tall as me." She turned back to the tree. "It's beautiful," she said.

"It sure is," said Papa.

"I like it too," said Mama.

Baby Brother clapped his hands. "It's . . ."

"Just right," finished Little Bunny with a smile.

Papa grinned. "I think we've found our tree," he said.

"Yay!" said the rest of the family. They paid Mr. Samson for the tree and took it home.

That evening, Little Bunny and her family began to decorate the tree.

Little Bunny was able to put the star on top all by herself.

When the family was done decorating,
they all stood back to admire the tree lights.

"Ooh," they said, as the lights glowed red
and green and gold.

Mama and Papa picked up Little Bunny and Baby Brother and kissed them. "You know, Little Bunny," said Papa, "that little tree is about the prettiest Christmas tree I've ever seen. I'm so glad you spotted it."

"Me too," said Mama.

"Me too," said Baby Brother.

Little Bunny smiled. "Me too," she said.